Long-Distance Running

Diana Noonan

Contents

Running Is a Sport for Everyone 2
Growing Up and Going Further 9
Extreme Running 14
The Marathon des Sables 18
Glossary 23
Index 24

Running Is a Sport for Everyone

Sport is often thought of as a team game.
But many sports involve just one person.
Long-distance running is one of them.

Both children and adults can enjoy long-distance running.
It is a sport for people
who want to compete in events,
and for people who like to run for fun and fitness.

Whatever **goals** a runner has,
there is a long-distance running event to suit them.

Think and Talk About ...

It is very important that runners drink plenty of water and avoid running in the hottest part of the day.

Children and adults sometimes take part in long-distance runs together.

Cross-Country Runs

Many children first try long-distance running
when they take part in a cross-country run at school.
Cross-country events are run over uneven ground.
Runners may have to cross fences
and run up and down hills.
Sometimes they have to splash through water and mud,
and run over rough ground.

Cross-country runs for children are from 800 metres
to 3 kilometres long.
The length of the run will depend
on the age of the runner.

Cross-country runners often have to run over muddy ground.

UP&RUNNING
NEWBURY BORDER LEAGUE
400

Community Clubs

Children who enjoy long-distance running at school usually join a running club in the community.

Runners meet after school or at weekends. The members are put into groups according to their age. They take part in long-distance road or cross-country runs.

An adult runner goes with each group of children to make sure everyone is safe. Club members often wear a uniform.

Community running clubs sometimes hold races for their members.

Think and Talk About ...

Community running clubs are often called "harrier clubs". Harrier clubs are named after a game of chase. The game was played over 180 years ago by children in England.

Fun runs are great for all ages.

Fun Runs

There are many long-distance running events for children and adults to take part in. They are generally called "fun runs".

Some events are to help raise money for **charities**. Other events are to **encourage** children to get fit.

In some long-distance events, families enter as a team. They run together or in a **relay**.

Growing Up and Going Further

Many adults enjoy long-distance running. Some people train by running to and from work or during their lunch time.

Others use a **treadmill** at home or at the gym. Weekends are a good time for taking part in a longer run of one-and-a-half hours or more.

Using a treadmill is an excellent way to train for long-distance running events.

Events to Aim For

Entering a special event
gives runners a reason to keep training.

The most common long-distance events for adults
are the 10-kilometre,
half marathon (just over 21 kilometres)
and full marathon (42.2 kilometre) runs.

It can take a beginning runner two or three months
to train for a half marathon,
and over four months to train for a full marathon.

Running Takes You Places

Long-distance runners usually take part in events
in their own country.
But, sometimes, runners may travel
to a special, famous event in another country.

Think and Talk About ...

People who compete in China's Great Wall Marathon must run up more than 5000 steps.

Famous Long-Distance Events

The Big Five Marathon takes place in South Africa. Runners cross the Entabeni Game Reserve. As they run, they frequently see big animals, such as giraffes and rhinoceroses.

Runners in the New York City Marathon run through one of the most exciting cities in the world.

In the Great Wall Marathon, runners run along the Great Wall of China.

The Great Wall Marathon in China is held every year.

43329
Multiple Sclerosis Society
IAN
DAVE
AGATHA

Fun on the Run!

Runners who take part in famous long-distance runs usually have a lot of fun.
People who come to watch them have fun, too.

The New York City Marathon has over 100 different bands playing along the running route.

In the London Marathon, many runners run in fancy dress. They dress up as **superheroes**, dinosaurs and even giant fruits.

Runners in the London Marathon sometimes dress as their favourite characters.

Think and Talk About ...

The oldest person to ever complete a marathon was 100 years old.

Extreme Running

Ultra Marathons

Some long-distance runners prefer an extra-big challenge. They find it by running an ultra marathon. An ultra marathon is any event that is longer than a marathon.

There are three main types of ultra marathon: distance events, time events and tough-**terrain** events.

Think and Talk About ...

The most common ultra marathons are 50 kilometres long. Others may be 100 or more kilometres long.

Some runners take part in longer events, such as the Copper Canyon Ultra Marathon in Mexico.

The Tough-Terrain Ultra Marathon

Long-distance runs can take place almost anywhere. Some of the most difficult runs take place in dangerous areas.

The Jungle Ultra takes place in Peru, in South America. Runners start in the mountains and run down, then through the Amazon jungle. They cross over 70 rivers and streams. They run through swarms of biting bugs. The run is almost 230 kilometres long!

Other difficult ultra marathons are through the hottest, driest, highest and coldest places in the world.

Competitors in the Jungle Ultra Marathon, Peru, run through rivers and streams.

Not everyone chooses long-distance running as their sport. But those who do, often never want to stop! Luckily, there are events to suit every age and ability.

Think and Talk About ...

Runners in a "time ultra marathon" run for a set length of time, such as 12 hours or more. The runner who runs the greatest distance in the set time is the winner.

The Marathon des Sables

The Marathon des Sables is one of the most famous extreme long-distance running events in the world. This event is famous for its distance and for where it takes place. It is known as the race where you carry everything you need on your back!

The Marathon des Sables is about 250 kilometres long. It takes place each April in the Sahara Desert, in Morocco. Runners have six days to run the race but one day is for having a rest.

Each day, runners take everything they need with them. They carry these supplies in a pack on their back. Inside the pack are water, food, a first-aid kit, and a map and compass. They also take a sleeping bag and sleeping mat.

Each night, the runners sleep in a tent.

Marathon des Sables competitors have to wear clothing that gives them protection from the sun.

It is very hot in the desert.
The temperature can be over 45° C during the day.

Sometimes, the sand is so deep that runners cannot run.
They have to walk.
Markers show the runners which way to go, but sometimes, they still have to use their map.

Some markers have special lights so runners can find their way after dark.

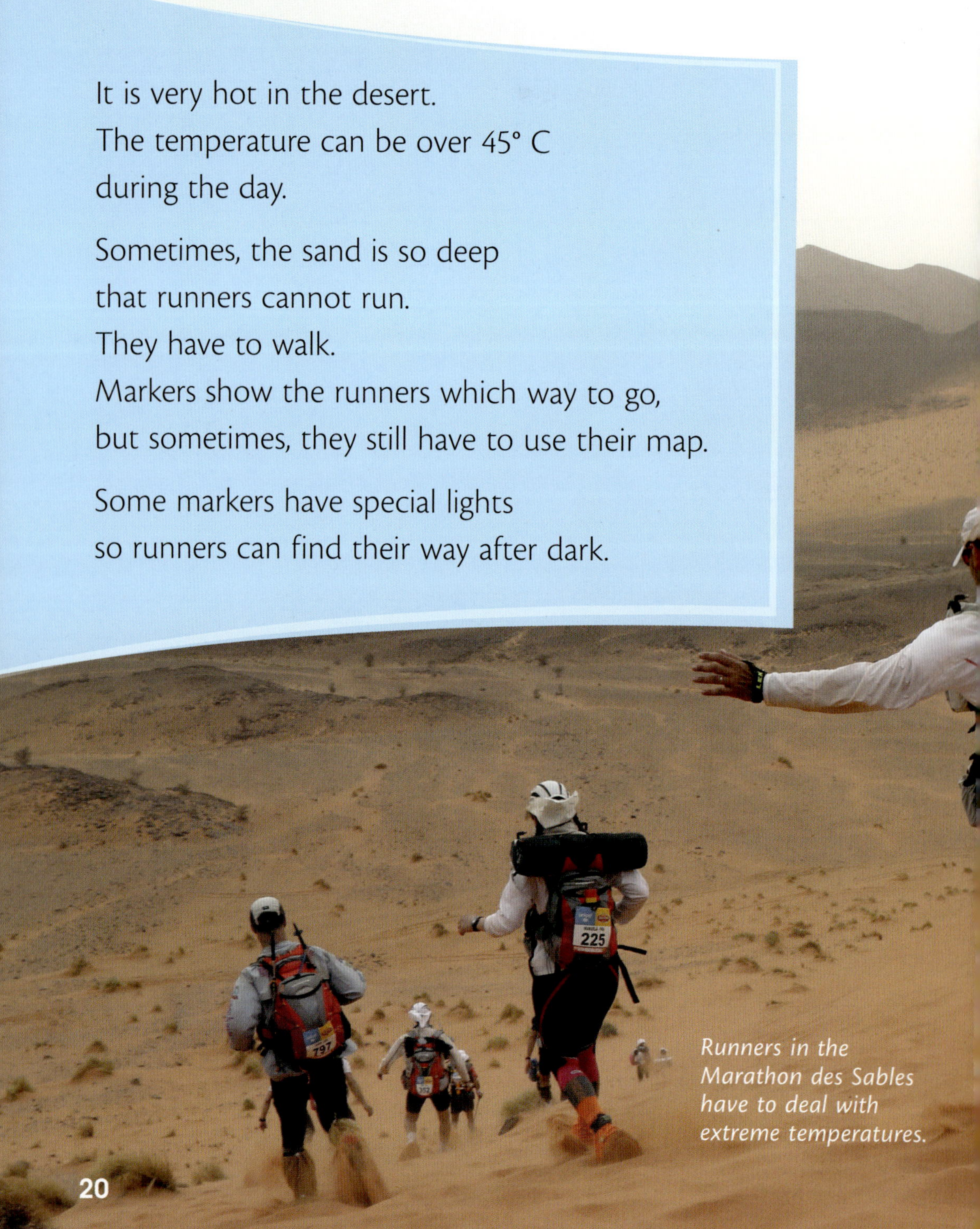

Runners in the Marathon des Sables have to deal with extreme temperatures.

286

Marathon des Sables runners
run up and down desert mountains.
They may even run through **sandstorms**.

The race is one of the world's most difficult
but, each year, more than 1000 people enter it.
Once a runner has finished the Marathon des Sables,
they know they can do almost anything!

Glossary

charities (*noun*)	groups that raise money to take care of people who need help
encourage (*verb*)	to give someone support when they are doing an activity
goals (*noun*)	challenges you set for yourself
relay (*noun*)	a race where members of a team take turns to run
sandstorms (*noun*)	clouds of sand blown up by the wind
superheroes (*noun*)	characters from books or films with special powers
terrain (*noun*)	the shape or features of a surface of land
treadmill (*noun*)	a machine that helps you run or walk on the spot

Index

Amazon jungle 16
Big Five Marathon 11
club 6–7
cross-country 4–6
desert 18–22
events 2–5, 8–11, 14–16, 18
fancy dress 12–13
fitness 2
fun runs 8
goals 2, 23
Great Wall Marathon 10–11
half marathon 10
London Marathon 12–13
Marathon des Sables 18–22
markers 20
mountains 16, 22
New York City Marathon 11, 13
relay 8, 23
supplies 18
terrain 14–16, 23
treadmill 9, 23
ultra marathon 14–17
uniform 6–7